EVICTED!

THE STRUGGLE FOR THE RIGHT TO VOTE

ALICE FAYE DUNCAN
ART BY **CHARLY PALMER**

CALKINS CREEK
AN IMPRINT OF ASTRA BOOKS FOR YOUNG READERS
New York

In loving memory of
Matie Armstrong Geter,
Golden Motley Jamerson, and
Minnie Harris Jameson
—AFD

Thank you to my wife, Dr. Karida Brown,
for stepping into the role of cheerleader
that my mother left vacant in 2009.
You are such an amazing person.
—CP

Ernest C. Withers's photograph of a Tent City family in 1960

Acknowledgments

In 2006, Ernest Withers gifted me a photography book about the Tent City Movement. His images demanded that I write about this history for young people. Baba Withers was long gone when I approached the research with serious intention in 2018. I set out on a journey to find farmers and activists who took part in the Tent City Movement of 1959. This book is possible because strangers accepted my phone calls and spoke with me like kinfolk. They invited me to their Somerville homes and shared family photo albums to help me capture the souls of the subjects. I am eternally grateful to the Towles Family. Ms. Erma, Ms. Bridget, Mr. Levearn, and Mr. Freddie painted vivid memories of Shephard "Papa" Towles. And as the first mother to settle in Tent City with her husband and children, Mrs. Mary Williams let me record several interviews as she recalled the indignity of sharecropping and the sacrifices her family made to vote. Under the direction of Executive Director Daphene R. McFerren, daughter of John and Viola McFerren, the Benjamin Hooks Institute for Social Change works with the University of Memphis to collect Tent City photographs and artifacts that directed the chronology of my book. And with ceaseless expressions of respect, I offer my abounding gratitude to Mr. James Jamerson Jr. With his treasure trove of family pictures and a heart dedicated to civil rights, his interviews inspired and spirited me from the book's harrowing beginning to its hopeful finish. Last, I want to pay my respect and gratitude to the founding members and leaders of The Original Fayette County Civic and Welfare League (OFCCWL). They serve as paragons of vision, initiative, and persistence. In these pages, I remember their struggle and celebrate their sacrifice.

—AFD

There's no royal blood a'coursing in my veins,
No great family background for me remains;
I haven't had a chance as others have had,
My living conditions have been kind'a bad;
But, it makes no difference what folks think or say,
I'M DETERMINED TO BE SOMEBODY, SOMEDAY.

—William Herbert Brewster

Mapping a Movement

Here is Fayette County, Tennessee, marked on a map. In 1950, it was the third largest land area in the state and third poorest county in the nation.

Fayette County's population of 28,000 was two-thirds Black, and the Black majority was made up mostly of unlearned sharecroppers* living on cotton farms owned by white landowners. While it was lawful for all adults to vote in public elections, the white ruling class in Fayette used the terror of fire and lynching to render Blacks powerless by suppressing Black voting and discouraging Black participation in the electoral process. The county's list of registered Black voters showed less than thirty names. But in 1959, after the legendary trial of sharecropper Burton Dodson, an uprising swept through the county like a forceful wind. This historical period is called the Fayette County Tent City Movement. Examining this period of American history reveals the power of what is possible when people unite to challenge injustice and make freedom a reality for all.

*Sharecroppers were farmers who paid for seed, tools, and a place to live not with money but with a "share" of the crops they raised on the landowners' farms. Most sharecroppers were Black, uneducated, and frequently cheated of their wages from white landowners, who exploited the defenseless workers.

Tent City Profiles

JAMES "JUNIOR" JAMERSON (1949–)
An abandoned child in Fayette County

BABY ANN JAMERSON
(1950–1956)
Junior's little sister

GOLDEN JAMERSON
(1898–1967)
Junior's paternal
grandmother

BURTON
DODSON
(1880–1968)
A farmer
accused
of murder

JAMES FRANK "JF" ESTES
(1919–1967)
A civil rights lawyer
from Memphis

JOHN MCFERREN
(1924–2020)
A Tent City leader
and grocer

VIOLA MCFERREN
(1931–2013)
A Tent City leader
and John's wife

HARPMAN JAMESON
(1925–2009)
A Tent City activist and
John's best friend

MINNIE JAMESON (1924–2009)
A Tent City activist and Harpman's wife

SHEPHARD TOWLES
(1907–1985)
A Tent City landowner
and farmer

ERNEST WITHERS
(1922–2007)
A famous Black
American
photographer

EARLIE B. WILLIAMS
(1935–2012)
The very first Tent
City resident

MARY WILLIAMS
(1937–)
Earlie's wife and
Tent City resident

CHARLIE BUTTS
(1942–)
Student volunteer from
Oberlin College

Contents

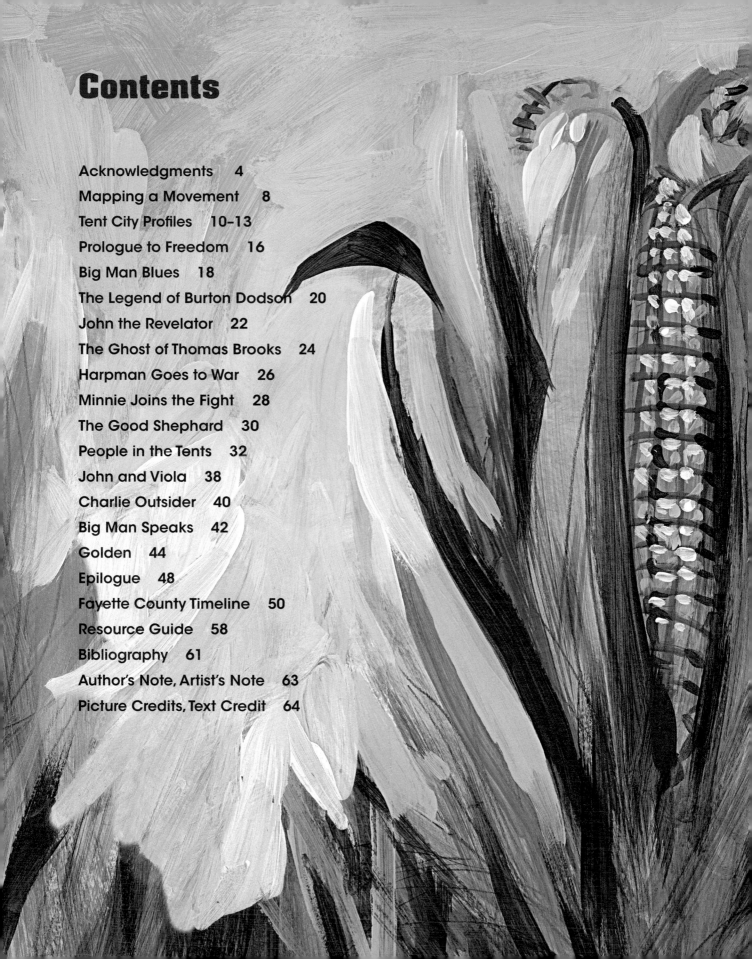

Prologue to Freedom

This is the story of a battle, a boy, and his broken-hearted blues. It is James Junior's journey through turbulent times in Fayette County, Tennessee. The people in Fayette County lived apart. Black and white children went to separate schools. Jim Crow signs hung high.

And while Black hands in Fayette were *free* to pick the cotton and corn, the same Black hands were barred from casting ballots in public elections. Black laborers lived as a voiceless people on the rural plains of West Tennessee. And if they dared to vote, they grappled with a dreaded question: What violence would they suffer from the Ku Klux Klan or White Citizens' Council?

Black landowners like John McFerren and Harpman Jameson swallowed their fear of death. They organized registration drives to help Black citizens vote in Somerville, the county seat. This struggle for freedom in Fayette County unleashed great evil. White farmers booted Black sharecroppers off the land, and Black babies were born in tents. James Junior wrestled with grief. Terror and gunshots reigned. But, the voiceless did finally speak. They even sang a freedom song.

Call out the names of men, women, and children from this Fayette County movement.

Record their conquering civil rights struggle for generations to come. Remember it. Pass it *on.*

Big Man Blues

The year was 1954. James Junior learned about love and loss before he learned to read. His mama and daddy would work all week and drink all Friday night. Before leaving her children alone, Dorothy would kiss James Junior and say, "Take care of Baby Ann."

James Junior was only five and Baby Ann was three when James Senior would pat the boy's head on Friday nights and say, "You our Big Man now!" Then the parents would hitch a ride from Fayette County to Beale Street in Memphis. And when Baby Ann cried from hunger, James Junior fed her day-old biscuits. When Baby Ann cried from fear because the house was cold and dark, Junior rocked her in his arms until she fell asleep.

One Friday night in July turned into Sunday morning. Their parents had not returned. Baby Ann lay on the patchwork quilt and groaned from one of her headache spells. "I want mama," she cried.

"Mama gone," huffed Junior as he turned to face the wall. Who could he call for help with no phone in the cropper shack? The boy prayed for Uncle Harpman, his daddy's brother, to knock on the door. He prayed for Aunt Minnie, his uncle's wife, to come in with plates of food.

RAP-TAP-TAP! His grandmother knocked. A grumbling in her feeble mind made her remember the children. She stood on the porch in a blue work jacket, and mismatched brogan boots. She wore a crumpled old church hat with a silver cross around her neck. Golden was her name.

When Mama Golden opened the unlatched door and shuffled toward the bed, James Junior shot up to hug her with all his strength. Baby Ann stretched out her arms for Golden to pick her up. Golden helped the children button their clothes over frayed pajamas. She tied their scuffed-toe shoes, and they all sat on the bed, watching black storm clouds gather and waiting on a savior.

Golden could not tell the future through the cracks in her feeble mind. But when it came to Harpman Jameson, her understanding was clear as rain. Her oldest son would search the county roads for her and receive the children. He would feed the lambs, raise them up, and love them like a father.

The Legend of Burton Dodson

James Junior understood that most bedtime stories don't carry a bit of truth. But, according to his Uncle Harpman, the legend of Burton Dodson was a Fayette County fact.

Reverend Dodson was a sharecropper back in 1940. It was rumored a white farmer challenged him about a woman they both loved. After Dodson served a lashing and left the farmer in the dirt, one hundred white men surrounded his shack to lynch his black body. Dodson ordered his brood of children to fall to the ground. Then he kicked the door open and ran through the night firing bullets to protect his life.

The white mob shot guns from bushes, trees, and the roof of an old smokehouse. Burton Dodson was hit five times, but his quick feet never stumbled. The preacher bolted from Fayette County and ran fifty miles to Memphis, where he hitched a ride to Chicago. Then he settled down in East St. Louis, Illinois.

Olin B. Burrow, a white deputy sheriff, was killed in the wild crossfire. The mob pinned his murder on Dodson, who never ran in Olin's direction.

"How did dat coon get away?" marveled men in the mob. Burton Dodson lived proud and free for the next eighteen years. And as the legend of his miraculous survival spread across the cotton fields, Black children in Fayette County would boast and brag, "I'm *bad* like Burton Dodson!"

Authorities captured Dodson in 1958 and shuttled him back to Tennessee. He stood trial for murder in 1959 at the dusty Somerville Court-house. For the first time ever, a Black lawyer tried a case in Fayette County, and Black farmers filled the seats to watch J. F. Estes defend Burton Dodson. Estes searched the court to pick Black jury members. But most were not registered voters and they could not serve as jurors.

Farmer John McFerren, who had piercing gray eyes, sat in court for the entire trial. The Black laborer bristled when the jury sent Burton Dodson to jail. John, with his steely gaze, caught a vision during the trial. He huddled Black men into a corner and boomed, "Our justice is the BALLOT BOX."

And while Burton Dodson served his sentence for a crime that he did not do, John McFerren drafted a plan to register Black voters and start a freedom movement.

John the Revelator

Burton Dodson was famous Fayette County lore, while John McFerren lived on the outskirts of Somerville as an ordinary man. He was a farmer, husband, and daddy to Little John and Jacqueline.

Born in 1924, John quit eighth grade when his daddy took sick. He put aside dreams of building motors and fixing cars to help his mama run their cotton farm. Then came World War II. The army drafted John, and he helped America and the Allied Forces defeat Adolf Hitler.

In the war, John used his small, quick body to move weapons to the front line. He raised bridges over rivers and lakes. Nobody sent Allied troops to help John overthrow Jim Crow when he returned to Fayette County in 1945.

McFerren is a noble name like Kennedy and King. It can mean liberator, activist, or inspired revelator. Fayette County denied Black citizens voting rights from the days of Reconstruction until the Dodson case, when John answered freedom's call. He formed the Fayette County Civic and Welfare League (FCCWL) and served as its president.

With guidance from attorney Estes and donations from Black landowners, like his best friend Harpman Jameson, John and the League drafted a charter to wield collective power and increase Black voters in Fayette County. Urging Black Americans to reject segregation and register to vote was revolutionary in the rural South.

"RECKLESS!" cried Viola McFerren. She feared for her husband's life as John crisscrossed white people's land to recruit Black tenants to join his struggle.

Everybody in Fayette County heard whispers about some loud firecracker, visiting cropper shacks and pushing Black folks to vote. Nobody expected such sparks from John, who quit grade school and was *no* polished talker.

The Ghost of Thomas Brooks

My talk ain't polished. Listen anyway.

This is my body. Battered and bruised. See my bulging eye.

Call me Tom Brooks. Here and not here. I am the wind.

Click! Click! A crowd of grinning white folk snap my picture.

Kodak Brownie cameras cost two dollars. It is April 1915.

My cracked black boots and broken Black limbs

Dangle from the trestle of a railroad bridge in Somerville.

I killed a rich white farmer and his helper. They say.

They say so much that ain't true. *Click! Click!*

Pictures tell the story as buzzing white children

Chirp with glee. They is so happy to miss a day of school

And dance in circles at the hanging of a niggra. *Me.*

My story ain't polished. Read it anyway.

Study my broken body like a book. Remember my blues.

Here and not here. I am wind, rain, and beloved son.

Colored folk was the majority in Fayette County, Tennessee.

We stayed on the land and picked cotton after slavery days.

We was cheated paupers in plantation shacks. Sharecroppers.

Colored men did not vote in 1915 or beyond. Not in Fayette County!

My muted tongue and broken Black body is a message down the

Dusty tracks of time. What is the lesson for my wounded soul?

Go make some white folk mad or "do good," like open a grocery,

Learn yourself to read, or cast your ballot as a first-class citizen.

It ain't no secret. THEY WILL KILL YOU.

Harpman Goes to War

Harpman Jameson heard stories about lynching from his grand-daddy—Albert Geter.

When Harpman turned six in 1931, he learned how Tom Brooks died on a county bridge. When he turned eighteen, Harpman left Fayette County to fight in World Wall II. When he turned twenty, Albert Geter died. The war ended, and Harpman returned home—an American with no vote.

Harpman married Minnie Harris in 1948. She was Viola McFerren's older sister. Harpman loved Minnie's sweet voice and her delight in books and learning. He hoped for a child to inherit her ways. In the meantime, the great tower of a farmer raised cattle, grew a rainbow of vegetables, and helped his pal, John McFerren, charter the Fayette County Civic and Welfare League in 1959.

Why stand with John and his freedom-hungry league? Harpman was a navy veteran, who wanted to exercise his

voting rights. There was also that distressing matter of his adopted children, James Junior and Baby Ann. Ann's headache spells persisted, and she died in 1956. Her death shook Harpman. And with his little girl gone, there was nothing else to lose and everything to gain, when he signed up for John McFerren's civil rights struggle.

Fatherhood made Harpman see himself with brand-new eyes. How could he fight for America in World War II and not fight for James Junior's right to vote?

"Let me tell you something," Harpman would declare over dinner. "A man and woman don't have no country if they don't have no vote."

Seated around the table with Harpman, Minnie, and Mama Golden, James Junior would register his uncle's sharp gaze. The boy could offer no reply, as the death of Baby Ann had snatched his voice away. And to compound his grief, Junior's longing for his "real" mama and daddy cast a permanent shadow of gloom over his golden face.

27

Minnie Joins the Fight

Minnie Jameson was no war veteran. She went to college and worked as a teacher.

When Minnie joined the League and registered her name to vote, the Fayette County School Board canceled her job. Losing employment changed Minnie. Her sweet purr turned to a fighting spirit. And while Harpman bellowed over bowls of steamy collards and yams about Negro voting rights, Minnie would declare, "That school board can take my job, but they cannot take my self-respect."

The Fayette County Civic and Welfare League voted Minnie secretary. Harpman served as treasurer. James Junior was a quiet son, who listened with his eyes during loud League rallies at Mount Olive Church. Since Minnie and Harpman never conceived a baby, James Junior was their only child. And as the couple raised their voices at the late-night rallies, *FREEDOM* was their battle cry.

The League members' strategy was to canvas the fifteen county districts and enlist potential Black voters. The strategy worked. Droves of Black men and women lined up to register at the Somerville courthouse. Wednesday was registration day.

Like Minnie, Black teachers risked termination by the white school board when they registered. And Black sharecroppers lost wages as they left the fields to be greeted by gangs of white folk, who cursed, threw rocks, and poured hot coffee in Black faces to suppress their will to vote.

During a primary election in 1959, white poll workers told Harpman and John it was an all-white election and no colored could vote. White workers blocked the men from entering the polls.

With haste, attorney Estes helped the League file a federal lawsuit for illegal treatment and obstruction of Black voters. The League's bravery prompted some white landowners to retaliate. After cotton was harvested that fall, they evicted registered Black tenants from the land.

Entire families were forced out of their homes when Black parents registered to vote in Fayette County. James Junior did not fear eviction. Minnie and Harpman owned their farm and a four-room house with electricity, a telephone, and a TV, but no indoor plumbing. The isolated property sat in the woods, one mile off Highway 76 in the Williston community.

While his shelter was sure, James Junior worried for friends. He was especially fearful for Jo Nell Johnson, a girl in his fifth-grade class. Her parents had seven children and worked for a white landlord with an evil reputation.

One evening as Junior walked the lonely path home from school and whizzing snow cleaved to his hat and coat, he followed rabbit tracks along the trail and posed a question to the listening trees.

"If the Johnsons go register, what's gonna happen to poor Jo Nell?"

The Good Shephard

Courage awakened many hearts after the League filed a lawsuit. During one registration day, a thousand Black sharecroppers converged on the courthouse wearing Sunday clothes. They rose before daylight to wait in line for many hours. The White Citizens' Council, a group of segregationists, used economic reprisals to punish these men and women who added their names to the voting roster.

The White Citizens' Council made a "blacklist" of registered Black voters and shared it widely. Pandemonium whipped through Fayette County like a tornado as white merchants copied the list and denied groceries and gasoline to registered Black customers. White doctors denied medicine to Black patients. White insurance agents canceled policies held by Black landowners with houses and cars. Farmers like Jo Nell's parents, were evicted from shacks, already uninhabitable with holes in the walls.

Shephard "Papa" Towles was one of the few Black landowners in Fayette. With two hundred acres, he invited displaced families to pitch army surplus tents in his field on Old Macon Road. Gertrude Beasley was an elderly Black woman who hosted families on her Fayette County property along Highway 57.

Mary and Earlie B. Williams and their son and three daughters were the first family to move into a tent on Papa Towles's land. They were evicted from the Leatherwood farm at Christmastime in 1960. Mary and her family slept in coats as they braved the bitter winter.

In January 1961, there was a rapid clip of evictions in Fayette and nearby Haywood County as more Black tenants registered. Seven hundred Black families in both counties combined were removed from farms where they had lived and worked for two and three decades. Evictions sparked a great migration of families from Fayette County to bunk in crowded shacks with kin or live in tents with mud under their feet.

While Papa Towles could not lodge every homeless family, he added to his property thirteen canvas tents purchased from an anonymous white merchant. Sixty children lived on his land with thirty mothers, fathers, grandparents, uncles, and aunts. During TV broadcasts and in national newspapers, the makeshift community was called "Tent City."

People in the Tents

A caravan of sharecroppers moved to the tents,
Bringing their possessions on the back of
Clunking trucks and mule-drawn wagons.

They settled in Tent City with yelping stray dogs,
Wood-burning stoves, potbelly wash kettles, oil lamps,
Patchwork quilts, and broken chests of drawers
Filled with knickknack memories.

The white tent merchant required anonymity for his safety,
While families in the tents owned blacklisted names like
Williams, Turner, Trotter, Junkins, Frazier, and Mason.
Their hiding place was a cross of unmerited suffering.

34

John McFerren needed help to spread the dire news.
Ernest Withers photographed the evicted families.
John wanted eyes to witness the pain of Black folks
Struggling to live and vote in Fayette County—USA.

CLICK!
CLICK! CLICK!
CLICK! CLICK! CLICK!

Mary, Earlie B., and their doe-eyed babies did not smile.
Standing at their tent in scrubbed, secondhand clothes,
They were a weary people—poor, proud, and persevering.
A Rolleiflex camera captured their courage in black and white.

When Viola McFerren visited with Mary in the tents,
Her steadfast fortitude mirrored Viola's rising commitment.
And when the *New York Post* sent a Black man to report the story,
Viola certainly had to marvel at John's rousing movement.

The Federal Justice Department sent FBI agents to
Investigate the area's long tradition of voter suppression.
Fayette County news reached Dr. Martin Luther King Jr.
Pictures of Tent City crossed President Kennedy's desk.

John and Viola felt responsible for people in the tents.
The sharecroppers did not register to be put outdoors,
Now their hungry families needed food and clothing.
The McFerrens spoke across the nation, seeking aid.

CLICK!
CLICK! CLICK!
CLICK! CLICK! CLICK!

A surge of publicity drew more reporters to Fayette County.
Ebony magazine printed a pictorial exposition, and
Dr. King mailed the League a letter with a large donation.
President Kennedy sent large trucks loaded with food.

CLICK!
CLICK! CLICK!
CLICK! CLICK! CLICK!

Pictures of Mary and Earlie B. made the papers.
John McFerren's crusade was a lead story.
And as the news traveled around the globe,
Black and white allies joined John's struggle.

John and Viola

America followed the McFerrens in the headlines as help arrived in great numbers. Volunteer carpenters laid wood floors in the tents. Labor unions like the United Packinghouse Workers donated food. Virgie Hortenstine of Operation Freedom gave loans to registered Black landowners denied credit at the banks. And when a plea for aid was printed in *Jet* magazine, shoes, clothes, and money arrived from faraway states like California, New Jersey, New York, Pennsylvania, and Illinois.

John and attorney J. F. Estes could never agree on a system to receive and distribute the donations. John broke ties with Estes in 1961 and changed his group's name to The Original Fayette County Civic and Welfare League (OFCCWL).

The split with Estes did not shatter John's vision. And as registered Black voters increased, so did incidents of violence. White terrorists fired guns at the Williams' tent on a frosty winter night. A bullet missed their sleeping baby and hit Earlie B. in the arm. John's family was a target too. White men threw bricks into his home. They chased his mother, Estella McFerren, off the road, and the aging woman wrecked her car in a ditch. In each case, white culprits were identified, but never charged.

Robert McFerren was John's baby brother. The college graduate moved away to avoid physical harm and economic retaliation. With Robert gone, John rented his brother's grocery and gas station to serve Fayette County's Black community. White merchants in Fayette County would not sell John gas or food to stock his store. Through the week, he drove his 1955 Thunderbird with a set of four-barreled carburetors to Memphis. There he purchased meat, milk, and bread. On his drive home, John zipped and zoomed around county roads as white locals plotted unsuccessfully to ambush his car.

Viola married John in 1950—the year she graduated high school. She never dreamed that loving him would put her life in danger. During the voting struggle, she worried especially about the safety of her children. But with each morning, she knelt in prayer. Her determination strengthened and Viola was unflinching.

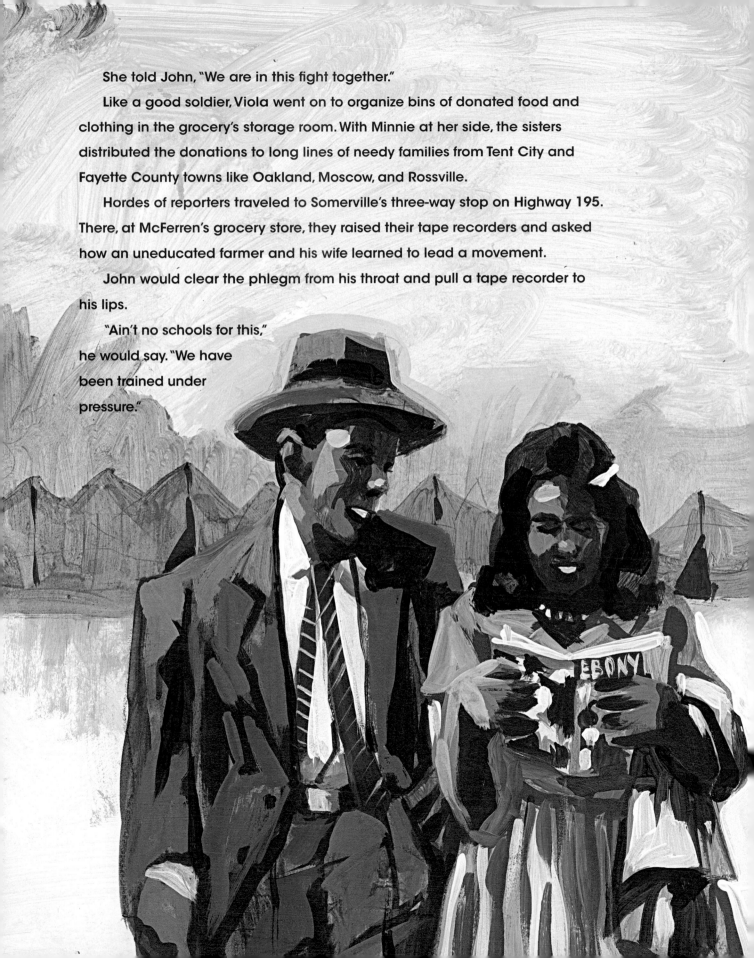

She told John, "We are in this fight together."

Like a good soldier, Viola went on to organize bins of donated food and clothing in the grocery's storage room. With Minnie at her side, the sisters distributed the donations to long lines of needy families from Tent City and Fayette County towns like Oakland, Moscow, and Rossville.

Hordes of reporters traveled to Somerville's three-way stop on Highway 195. There, at McFerren's grocery store, they raised their tape recorders and asked how an uneducated farmer and his wife learned to lead a movement.

John would clear the phlegm from his throat and pull a tape recorder to his lips.

"Ain't no schools for this," he would say. "We have been trained under pressure."

Charlie Outsider

A white student from Oberlin College canceled summer fun when he read the news about Tent City. Charlie Butts packed his bags and drove all night from Ohio to Tennessee. On his arrival, he worked as a League volunteer. Charlie studied the grassroots movement through the lens of his college books. Something was missing. Many in the Black community did not own telephones, and the League needed some way to share urgent information about protest marches, voting, and late-night rallies.

One morning as the two broke Jim Crow traditions and worked together in the League's rickety headquarters, Charlie asked Minnie, "Would you consider writing a weekly newsletter?"

Minnie had no objection. "Who will teach me how?" she asked.

The League's donated mimeograph machine was a mystery to her.

"I WILL!" Charlie pointed both thumbs at himself. And for the duration of his stay, he taught Minnie how to type, make mimeo copies, and publish the *League Link*.

When Charlie returned to college, Minnie carried on as *League Link* editor, and two years later, good news arrived. Under John Doar, the Justice Department's Civil Rights Division filed a lawsuit to block white landowners from evicting Black sharecroppers because they had registered to vote. A consent agreement was filed, and white landowners agreed to stop evictions in July 1962.

Peals of praise rang from tent to tent as families gathered to read the *League Link* in the summer of 1962. A breeze of relief seemed to blow across the county. No new families moved into the tents, and several white merchants resumed business and services to Black registered voters.

With the consent agreement filed, white landowners began to purchase expensive farm equipment to avoid hiring a cheap labor force that pressed for equal rights. With no new opportunities to work, one by one, tent families began to pack up their memories and moved to nearby counties like Shelby, Chester, and Madison. While Papa Towles pulled down tents, John McFerren made big plans to pick a Black political candidate and help that candidate *win.*

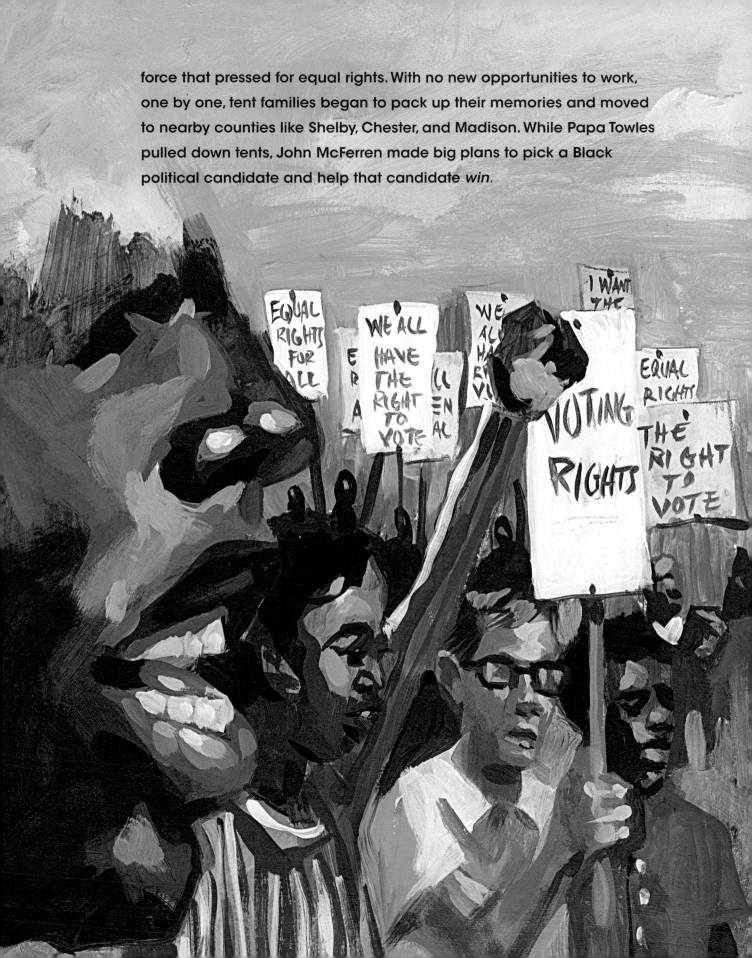

Big Man Speaks

The year was 1963. As John McFerren searched for brave candidates to run in the Fayette County elections, Dr. King marched on Washington, DC, to terminate Jim Crow laws and demand better schools, jobs, and housing for every American citizen.

James Junior, with his sad-eyed smile, worked the counter at McFerren's grocery in 1963. Each day after school, he furtively feasted on the political talk of the chatty customers while he bagged their groceries, and replied with only a "please come again," or, "thank you very much."

The quiet teenager did not talk civil rights with Harpman, Minnie, or Mama Golden—but he perceived the changing times. The evidence was on TV. He saw Black children march for equal rights in Birmingham. He saw dogs attack the children. He saw the children put in jail. And in 1964, he saw President Lyndon B. Johnson sign the Civil Rights Act to abolish segregation, with Dr. King at his side.

Fifty white college kids from New York found their way to Fayette County in the summer of 1964. Working with fiery League members like Square Mormon, in his porkpie hat, and Maggie Horton, with her megaphone voice, Cornell University students trudged across cotton fields to encourage voting in the Black community. With their help, the League also organized a campaign to elect Reverend June Dowdy, a Black man, for tax assessor and L. T. Redfearn, a white man, for sheriff.

Black Fayette County voters went to cast their ballots by the thousands on August 6, 1964. Official poll watchers saw white locals stuff the ballot boxes with countless illegal votes. The results? Preacher Dowdy and L. T. Redfearn both suffered defeat. But, the League moved forward. Their circle of allies grew, and more college activists descended on Fayette County in the spring of 1965.

It was the month of May when University of Chicago students joined the League in mass demonstrations. They marched through downtown Somerville to denounce lingering evils of segregation in Fayette schools, restaurants, and the local movie theater.

With his quiet manner and rail-thin frame, nobody invited James Junior to march or carry a protest sign. One day a fire in his feet lifted him from his old wooden desk and stack of tattered books. James Junior left school and ran for downtown Somerville to join the League and college kids. He heard footsteps and singing before he reached the crowd.

Woke up this morning with my mind stayed on freedom!
Walking and talking with my mind stayed on freedom!
Singing and praying with my mind stayed on freedom!
Hallelu—hallelu—hallelujah!

Gloom and grief took flight on wings as James Junior marched and opened his mouth to sing. Would he be punished for skipping school? Whatever the price, he was willing to pay it.

Golden

James Junior remembered 1965 with a furious clarity.
He recalled sitting on the couch beside grandma Golden.
Together they watched the news as white state troopers in Selma
Brutalized nonviolent activists on the Edmund Pettus Bridge.

John Lewis, a future US congressman, led the charge as
Six hundred students, clergy, and church folk demanded
Unhindered voting rights for all American citizens.
Junior and Golden winced at the bloody news footage.

CLICK! CLICK!

Photojournalists like Flip Schulke and Bruce Davidson
Put their lives in danger, too, on the Edmund Pettus Bridge.
They captured portraits of terror with Nikon and Leica cameras.
Black and white voices raged at the sight of helpless, beaten bodies.
The blood that spilled in Selma awakened sleepy public opinions.

CLICK! CLICK!

Photographs and newsreels needed no exposition.
James Junior and Golden exchanged no commentary.
They were connected souls who shared a silent understanding.
Selma was a growing seed—a sprawling voter movement
Planted first in 1959 across the cotton fields of Fayette County.

Finally, to serve Black America the unfettered freedom to vote—
President Lyndon Johnson signed the Voting Rights Act of 1965.
This law changed the face of local, state, and national elections as
Black Americans voted in record numbers and won political seats.

Four Black men and two Black women won Fayette County posts in 1966.
They were voted to serve on the county board with thirty magistrates.
The Black magistrates were disrespected for the full length of the term,
While each one served with dignity and a golden crown of courage.

As he considered the changing seasons and spirit of the times,
James Junior asked himself, "What is my contribution?"
He wanted to make a difference like Harpman and Minnie.
He wanted to offer some great sacrifice like John and Viola.

Junior took action without parental prodding in the fall of 1966.
He boarded a yellow school bus to integrate Fayette County High.
He expected shiny desks and books served with loud stinging threats.
Change agents endure hardships and Junior embraced the challenge.

White students with racist views troubled him with menacing taunts.
They assaulted him and his Black classmates with pushing in the halls.
Junior was pelted with pennies and nickels each day he rode the bus.
He studied his books, passed his tests and graduated in 1967.
CLICK! CLICK!

James Junior is a farmer now with grandbabies at his feet.
He pulls pictures from a worn shoebox to recall the Fayette movement.
His lambs ask constant questions about who, what, when, and *why*.
And James Junior speaks with authority. His memory is an open book.
He says the past is the present, and it is urgent they understand,
"Every life is a battlefield and freedom is a golden prize."

This voting advertisement was issued by the National Association for the Advancement of Colored People (NAACP) in the early to mid-1960s.

Epilogue

It is all of us, who must overcome the crippling legacy of bigotry and injustice. And we shall overcome.

—President Lyndon B. Johnson

The Voting Rights Act of 1965 was an effort to eliminate racial discrimination in America's political elections. The law was passed to stop such criminal acts as racial gerrymandering, poll taxes, and economic reprisals like those experienced by Black voters in Fayette County.

The power and potency of the Voting Rights Act was its "preclearance" requirement. Cities and states could not add or change voting laws without supervision and permission from the US Department of Justice. The Voting Rights Act was weakened in 2013, by the *Shelby County (AL) v. Holder* decision, when a majority of five Supreme Court Justices voted against the long-standing preclearance rule. With the removal of federal supervision, American voters and political elections are vulnerable to abuse and lawlessness.

Injustice remains as persistent a foe as it was in 1959. A great number of Americans struggle still to achieve equitable voting rights and fair political elections. More than fifty years after Black voters in Fayette County were evicted and reduced to living in muddy tents, voter suppression and intimidation continues in every corner of the nation.

Who will be like the daring men, women, and children from the fertile plains of Fayette County? They championed equality and justice for all. Despite his young age, James Junior served the freedom struggle with conquering faith and courage. He accepted the charge to rise and change history for good.

Today—it is your turn.

Now is your time.

In 1960, Ernest Withers took this photograph of Fayette County residents as they stood in line to apply for voter registration cards.

Fayette County Timeline

September 1957

Under the Civil Rights Act of 1957, the Justice Department formed a Civil Rights Division to prosecute anyone who conspired to deny another citizen the right to vote.

April 1959

Because of lynching and other forms of racial terror, Black Fayette County residents did not register to vote. With no registration on file, they could not serve on the jury when Burton Dodson, a Black man, was falsely charged with murder. The desire to be jurors and vote in public elections inspired John McFerren to form the Fayette County Civic and Welfare League. His group organized the first Black voter registration drive in the rural American South.

August 1959

Black farmers John McFerren and Harpman Jameson were turned away at the polls when they tried to vote in the Fayette County sheriff election.

November 1959

A Federal lawsuit was filed against the Fayette County Democratic Executive Committee charging it with refusing Black citizens the right to vote. It was the first lawsuit filed under the Civil Rights Act of 1957.

April 1960

The White Citizens' Council made a list of Black residents who had registered to vote in Fayette County. To suppress the mounting registration drive, the white council of merchants banned the Black registered voters from buying groceries or gasoline, and from receiving bank loans and medical services in Fayette County and surrounding areas in West Tennessee and North Mississippi.

June 1960

Charlie Butts was an Oberlin College student who visited Fayette County to volunteer with the League. He helped Minnie Jameson publish the *League Link*, a weekly newsletter that would go on to serve social, political, and economic news to the Black Fayette County community for thirty years.

August 1960

When the National Association for the Advancement of Colored People (NAACP) called for its 350,000 members to boycott Gulf, Esso, and Texaco, the gasoline companies discontinued their embargo and once again served Black customers in Fayette County. Also, Black journalist Ted Poston wrote about the suppression of Black Fayette County voters in the *New York Post*. His news articles helped to publicize the Fayette County Civil Rights Movement beyond Tennessee and drew a great surge of reporters to the Tent City site.

September 1960

More than a thousand Black voters were added to the Fayette County voting roster. When crops were harvested that season, white landowners evicted hundreds of Black sharecroppers because they had registered. Black landowner Shephard Towles welcomed many displaced families to his farm to live rent-free. While the League named the makeshift community Freedom Village, news reporters called it Tent City.

December 1960

Mary and Earlie B. Williams were evicted from the Leatherwood farm in Fayette County. Their white landlord dismissed the tenants because the couple exercised their legal rights and registered to vote. The Williamses were the first displaced family to occupy an army surplus tent on Shephard Towles's farm. The Tent City compound stood along "Old Macon Road," which is now called Highway 195.

Reecie Hunter Malone receives her voter registration card in Fayette County, 1960.

December 1960

The U.S. Department of Justice filed a lawsuit against forty-five landowners, twenty-four merchants, and the Somerville Bank and Trust because of the economic reprisals they inflicted upon Black Fayette County residents who registered to vote. And when Senator Estes Kefauver sent the Red Cross to help Black families in Tent City, the workers reported that evicted families required no assistance. National labor unions donated food, clothing, and money to the displaced families.

January 1961

During his press conference as the newly elected American president, John F. Kennedy learned about the social unrest, hunger, and violence in Fayette County from a news reporter. With encouragement from civil rights activist Ella Baker, Dr. Martin Luther King Jr. mailed the League an eight-hundred-dollar check to support Tent City families throughout the winter of 1961.

March 1961

John McFerren and the League broke ties with their Black attorney, J. F. Estes, when the two men could not agree on a system to distribute Tent City donations.

June 1961

Orville Freeman, secretary of agriculture, was authorized by President Kennedy to send food to Fayette and Haywood counties, as Black farmers in both counties experienced eviction when they registered to vote.

July 1962

A consent decree in federal court ended all lawsuits against the white landlords and merchants and the bank accused of economic reprisals against Black voters in Fayette County. This agreement required defendants to stop evictions against registered Black farmers. This judgment also released the defendants from court costs and any requirement to admit their guilt.

54

Tent City, December 1960

September 1962

One by one, families began to move from the tents to seek new horizons. They left as first-class citizens, who sacrificed wages and faced the possibility of starvation and death, for the right to vote. Some Tent City families, like those of Mary and Earlie Williams, went to farm in nearby Tennessee counties. Other families left the South completely and moved to New York and Chicago to try their fate in urban landscapes.

August 1963

College students from Cornell University visited Fayette County to help the League register more Black voters. During this summer, Dr. Martin Luther King Jr. and 250,000 activists marched on Washington to demand decent housing, employment, and schools for all Americans. Dr. King called for the abolishment of legal segregation and delivered his "I Have a Dream" speech on the steps of the Lincoln Memorial.

August 1964

Cornell University students returned to Fayette County to register Black voters and campaign for two League candidates, June Dowdy and L.T. Redfearn. Official poll watchers saw white locals stuff the ballot boxes with illegal votes. Dowdy lost the election for tax assessor and Redfearn lost his run for sheriff. However, there was a victory that summer when President Lyndon Johnson signed the Civil Rights Act of 1964. This legislation abolished legal segregation in America.

May 1965

Students from the University of Chicago volunteered in Fayette County. They joined forces with the League and marched through Somerville to protest the stronghold of segregation in Fayette County schools and restaurants.

June 1965

The McFerrens and other Black families successfully sued the Fayette County Board of Education and desegregated the local schools. The case is titled, *John McFerren, Jr., et al., v. Fayette County Board of Education.*

August 1965

President Johnson signed the Voting Rights Act. This monumental law was an effort to make voting free, fair, and accessible to all, with no regard to economic class or racial identity.

August 1966

Four Black men (William Hazlitt, Charlie Minor, Cooper Parks, Sherman Perry) and two Black women (Geraldine Johnson, Gladys Allen) were elected to the Fayette County Quarterly Court. While their service as county magistrates was not an easy adjustment, they shouldered the challenge to leave an example and pave a trail for younger generations born and yet to come.

September 1966

Without parental prodding, James Jamerson Jr. joined the initiative to desegregate the Fayette County Schools. He left the familiar environment of his Black school (W. P. Ware) to integrate Fayette County High. He was a twelfth-grade student. While frequently harassed by white classmates, James Junior stayed the course and graduated in 1967.

Resource Guide

BOOKS OF GENERAL INTEREST

Allen, James. *Without Sanctuary: Lynching Photography in America*. Santa Fe, NM: Twin Palms Publishers, 2014.

Bailey, Ronald W., ed. *Let Us March On!: Selected Civil Rights Photographs of Ernest C. Withers 1955–1968*. Boston: Massachusetts College of Art, 1992.

Cox, Julian. *Road to Freedom: Photographs of the Civil Rights Movement, 1956–1968*. Atlanta, GA: High Museum of Art, 2008.

Dowd, Douglas F. and Mary Nichols, editors. *Step by Step: Evolution and Operation of the Cornell Students' Civil-Rights Project in Tennessee, Summer, 1964*. New York: Published for the Fayette County Fund by W. W. Norton, 1965.

Martin, Spider. *Selma 1965: The Photographs of Spider Martin*. Austin, TX: University of Texas Press, 2015.

MUSIC

Fayette County by Pete Seeger (Acetate Label)

Freedom Highway—LIVE by the Staple Singers (Sony Records)

Harvest for the World by the Isley Brothers (Legacy Records)

Sing for Freedom—The Story of the Civil Rights Movement Through Its Songs (Smithsonian Folkways)

Songs My Mother Taught Me by Fannie Lou Hamer (Smithsonian Folkways)

DOCUMENTARY FILMS AND WEBSITES

Fayette County Tennessee (1964)

Nick Lawrence, Berkeley, CA, fine art photographer
View 56 black-and-white photographs taken in Fayette County during the summer of 1964. Cornell student Nick Lawrence used his Pentax camera to document the determined people, the lush land, and the harrowing struggle for voting rights. nicklawrencephotography.com/fayette-county-tenn.

Freedom's Front Line: Duty of the Hour

See and hear interviews with members of the Fayette County Civic and Welfare League. Interviews include the McFerrens, the Jamesons, and LeVearn Towles, the son of landowner, Shephard Towles. memphis.edu/dutyofthehour/documentaries/freedomsfrontline.php.

Ida B. Wells: Lynching at the Curve

See and hear scholars explore the life of Ida B. Wells, an American journalist who used investigative journalism to fight against lynching in Tennessee and across the American South during the early twentieth century. (youtube. com/watch?v=62eH6TNP72E)

Uplift the Vote: The Fayette County Civil Rights Movement

See and hear Fayette County activists speak about their struggles during the Tent City Voting Rights Movement. Interviews include John and Viola McFerren, Harpman and Minnie Jameson, and Earlie B. and Mary Williams. (youtube.com/watch?v=xh515oDkYeQ)

PLACES TO VISIT

Birmingham Civil Rights Institute
520 16th Street North
Birmingham, AL 35203
bcri.org

National Civil Rights Museum
450 Mulberry Street
Memphis, TN 38103
civilrightsmuseum.org

National Museum of African
American History and Culture
1400 Constitution Avenue, NW
Washington, DC 20560
nmaahc.si.edu

National Memorial for Peace and
Justice—Equal Justice Initiative
115 Coosa Street
Montgomery, AL 36104
museumandmemorial.eji.org

James "Junior" Jamerson in the fall of 1966 (left) and in the fall of 2018 (right)

Mary M. Williams was the first mother to move into Tent City with her children and husband, Earlie B. Willams.

Levearn Towles was a displaced sharecropper in 1960 and the son of Shephard Towles.

Bibliography

All quotations used in the book can be found in the following sources marked with an asterisk (*).

Bailey, Ronald W., ed. *Let Us March On!: Selected Civil Rights Photographs of Ernest C. Withers 1955–1968*. Boston: Massachusetts College of Art, 1992.

Benjamin L. Hooks Institute (memphis.edu/benhooks). "Allen Yancey on Burton Dodson, and Voting." YouTube, August 4, 2015, youtube.com/watch?v=Yh-q0ZfkZYQY.

_____. "Charlie Butts on Change Our Way of Life." YouTube, August 4, 2015, youtube.com/watch?v=EEQIItMLgms.

_____. "Charlie Butts on League Link." YouTube, August 4, 2015, youtube.com/watch?v=h3iZca46fhA.

_____. "Minnie Jameson on Charlie Butts and League Link." YouTube, August 4, 2015, youtube.com/watch?v=-yq9zRfN-GM.

"Cold War in Fayette County." *Ebony*, September 1960, 27–34.

Dowd, Douglas F. and Mary Nichols, eds. *Step by Step; Evolution and Operation of the Cornell Students' Civil-Rights Project in Tennessee, Summer, 1964*. New York: Published for the Fayette County Fund by W. W. Norton, 1965.

"Fayette Timeline 1949." The University of Memphis. memphis.edu/tentcity/movement/fayette timeline-1949.php.

Forman, James. *The Making of Black Revolutionaries: A Personal Account*. New York: Macmillan, 1972.

*Hamburger, Robert. *Our Portion of Hell: Fayette Country, Tennessee: An Oral History of the Struggle for Civil Rights*. New York: Links, 1973.

*Jamerson, James. "My Family and the Movement." Interview with the author, November 10, 2018. Somerville, TN.

*_____. "Remembering Mama Golden." Interview with the author, December 22, 2018. Somerville, TN.

*_____. "Skipping School for the Movement." Interview with the author, May 12, 2019.

Kelley, Eugene. *Tent City—Home of the Brave*. Pamphlet. AFL-CIO Industrial Union Department, 1960.

King, Martin Luther, Jr. "To James F. Estes." Draft letter, ca., 1960. The Martin Luther King, Jr. Research and Education Institute, Stanford University. kinginstitute. stanford.edu/king-papers/documents/james-f-estes.

Klein, Christopher. "Remembering Selma's 'Bloody Sunday.'" *HISTORY*, August 30, 2018. history.com/news/selmas-bloody-sunday-50-years-ago.

Leicaphila. "Bruce Davidson." December 26, 2015. leicaphilia.com/tag/ bruce-davidson.

"Negro Assassin Lynched by Mob." *Batesville Daily Guard*, April 29, 1915, 1.

"No Need For Fancy Shoes, Food in Tent City." *Jet*, January 19, 1961, 23.

Phillips, Steve. *Brown Is the New White: How the Demographic Revolution Has Created a New American Majority*. New York: The New Press, 2018.

Poinsett, Alex. "Negro Cleric Tried for Murder." *Jet*, April 16, 1959, 46.

Reed, Tyrone Tony. "Roots of John McFerren." *West Tennessee Examiner*, January 31, 2014, 4.

Saunders, Richard L. *Encouraged by a Little Progress: Voting Rights and the Contests Over Social Place and Civil Society in Tennessee's Fayette and Haywood Counties, 1958–1964*. University of Memphis, PhD diss., 2021.

_____. *"TENT CITY," TENNESSEE*. utm.edu/staff/accarls/civilrights/tent_city_history. html. *Tent City Timeline: The Civil Rights Struggle in Fayette County—October 1960—Civil Rights—A Jackson Sun Special Report*, orig.jacksonsun.com/civ-ilrights/sec4_timeline.shtml.

Schulke, Flip, and Robert S. Nemser. *He Had a Dream: Martin Luther King Jr. and the Civil Rights Movement*. New York: W. W. Norton, 1995.

Stokes, Thaddeus T. "Fayette County Farmers Suffer Economical Squeeze." *Memphis World*, February 17, 1960.

Towles, Freddie. "Everybody Called Him Papa." Interview with the author, February 18, 2019.

Towles, Levearn. "My Daddy Had Five Jobs (A Son Remembers Shephard Towels)." Interview with the author, October 19, 2018.

Travis, Fred. "The Evicted." *Reporting Civil Rights—Volume One (1941–1963)*, Library of America Classic Journalism, 2003, 541–549.

Williams, Mary. "Born in a Tent." Interview with the author, October 31, 2018.

_____. "We Wanted Work." Interview with the author, November 4, 2018.

Author's Note

I was born and raised in Tennessee. I am also the beneficiary of a public school education with degrees from the University of Memphis and the University of Tennessee at Knoxville. I wrote *Evicted!* to give students in Tennessee and across the nation an understanding of this valiant American history that must not be forgotten. May you remember with the urgency to never repeat past misdeeds. March ON!

—*AFD*

Artist's Note

It was an honor to illustrate *Evicted!* about the brave citizens of Fayette County, Tennessee. I found it painful to read the stories of the Tent City and even harder to paint. I can't imagine what it was like for them to live in those hard times. I dedicate this book to all the people who lived through what was an extremely difficult period in American history. I know you, I love you.

—*CP*

Alice Faye Duncan and Levearn Towles at the Tent City historical marker. His father, Shephard Towles, pitched tents on the family's land in 1960, and gave shelter to Black sharecroppers, evicted from rental homes when they registered to vote in Fayette County, Tennessee.

Picture Credits

Dr. Ernest C. Withers, Sr., courtesy of the WITHERS FAMILY TRUST: 4, 50, 53; Library of Congress, Prints and Photographs Division, LC-USZC4-10249: 48; Associated Press: 55; James Albert Jamerson Jr.: 60 (top left); Alice Faye Duncan, courtesy of James Albert Jamerson Jr.: 60 (top right); Alice Faye Duncan, courtesy of Mary M. Williams: 60 (bottom left); Alice Faye Duncan, courtesy of Levearn Towles: 60 (bottom right), 64; Tarrice Love: 63 (top); Steve West Photo: 63 (bottom).

Text Credit

Courtesy of the William Herbert Brewster Family: 7.

For information about permission to reproduce selections from this book, please contact permissions@astrapublishinghouse.com.

Calkins Creek
An imprint of Astra Books for Young Readers,
a division of Astra House Publishing
calkinscreekbooks.com

Printed in China

ISBN: 978-1-68437-979-8 (hc)
ISBN: 978-1-63592-565-4 (eBook)
Library of Congress Control Number: 2021906339

First edition
10 9 8 7 6 5 4 3 2 1

Design by Barbara Grzeslo
The text is set in ITC Avant Garde Gothic Demi.
The art is done in acrylic on illustration board.